Sarah F

STORYCATCHER

and Maskwa's Tipi Tales

Sarah Ponakey, STORYCATCHER and Maskwa's Tipi Tales

By Sita MacMillan

Illustrated by
Azby Whitecalf

annick press
toronto · berkeley

Cover art by Azby Whitecalf, designed by Sam Tse
Interior designed by Sam Tse

Edited by Stephanie Myers
Copy edited by Hope Masten
Proofread by Eleanor Gasparik
Cree language review by Dorothy Visser

Annick Press Ltd.

This book is funded in part by the Government of Canada. *Ce livre est financé en partie par le gouvernement du Canada.* We acknowledge the support of the Canada Council for the Arts. *Nous remercions le Conseil des arts du Canada de son soutien.* We would like to acknowledge the funding support of the Ontario Arts Council (OAC) and the Government of Ontario for their support. We also acknowledge the support of the Government of Ontario through the Ontario Book Publishing Tax Credit, and through Ontario Creates.

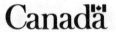

Library and Archives Canada Cataloguing in Publication

Title: Maskwa's tipi tales / written by Sita MacMillan ; illustrated by Azby Whitecalf.
Names: MacMillan, Sita, author. | Whitecalf, Azby, illustrator
Description: Series statement: Sarah Ponakey, storycatcher
Identifiers: Canadiana (print) 20240416422 | Canadiana (ebook) 20240416430 | ISBN 9781773219493 (hardcover) | ISBN 9781773219509 (softcover) | ISBN 9781773219516 (EPUB) | ISBN 9781773219523 (PDF)
Subjects: CSH: Cree—Social life and customs—Juvenile fiction. | LCGFT: Novels.
Classification: LCC PS8625.M57 M87 2025 | DDC jC813/.6—dc23

Published in the U.S.A. by Annick Press (U.S.) Ltd.
Distributed in Canada by University of Toronto Press.
Distributed in the U.S.A. by Publishers Group West.

Printed in Canada

annickpress.com
sitamacmillan.com
azbywhitecalf.com

MIX
Paper | Supporting
responsible forestry
FSC® C103567

Also available as an e-book. Please visit annickpress.com/ebooks for more details.

This book is dedicated to my daughter Avani:
may you continue to follow your dreams and
believe in life's magic. —S.M.

Thank you to all young girls who are keeping
our traditions alive! —A.W.

C✹NTENTS

GLSSARY

CREE WORD	ENGLISH MEANING
âhâsiw	crow
maskwa/maskwak	bear/bears
kôhkom	grandmother
anikwacās	squirrel
hiy hiy	thank you
mikiwap	tipi
Katawasisin.	It is beautiful.

tansi'	hello
Kîhtwâm ka-wâpamitin.	I will see you next time.
mêscacâkanis	coyote
wâposos	rabbit/bunny
Nehiyawak	the language of the Plains Cree

Dear Sarah!

I miss you!!! What have you been up to?

Eagle has been missing you too!! We have been busy in summer camps, but I tell everyone about you. I wish I could be there playing in the woods with you and Eden.

Do you get to eat fresh berries straight from the bushes? Have you been to a powwow?

Is Âhâsiw having fun over there? Has Eden taught you any fancy new words?

She has the best words!

Dear Sarah,

I miss you!!! What have you been up to?

Eagle has been missing you too!! We have been busy in summer camps, but I tell everyone about you. I wish I could be out there playing in the woods with you and Eden.

Do you get to eat fresh berries straight from the bushes? Have you been to a powwow? Is Âhâsiw having fun over there?

Has Eden taught you any fancy new words? She has the best words!

Have you seen any maskwak in the woods yet? Are they huge? As big as a car? I have SO many questions, but I don't have as much to share here. It's boring without you.

Miss you,

Arya

The Eden Mystery

I PUT ARYA'S LETTER IN THE SIDE pocket of my backpack next to Âhâsiw, who is safely tucked away. I throw my backpack over my shoulder and hop out of Kôhkom's old car. We're back from our last trip to town of the summer. These days my adventures with Âhâsiw have been helping Kôhkom and playing with Eden and her cousin Avani in the woods. My moccasins hit the ground, with a poof of dust rising up. I like watching the dry earth dance in the air when I walk on these dirt roads.

It's been fun being back in the woods with Kôhkom, even though I sure miss Arya. I've also been missing Eden these days! She has been too busy to hang out all week. Most weeks, Eden meets me at the car to help bring in the groceries, but not today. And last week Avani came to help instead.

Maybe I should write my last letter to Arya about this mystery?!

I love to watch the dust settle behind Kôhkom's car. Sometimes I draw silly pictures on the car and wait to see if they're still there when we drive into town again. As much as I enjoy picking out a treat after a long day of running errands in town, I can't wait to get back to spend time with Eden and Avani.

We have a system when we come back from these trips:

Right away, Kôhkom brings in the bag with the groceries that need to go into the freezer. (Don't want them to melt more than they already have!)

I bring the rest of the bags up the steps with Eden and into the front entrance to hand to Kôhkom.

I make sure Kôhkom's favorite magazine is sitting on the porch bench for when she rests.

I leave with Eden and Avani to hang out until the stars start to come out.

Except today, no Eden and no Avani. Hmmm ... definitely strange.

When I first arrived, Eden couldn't wait to see me and we were together all the time. This week, my last week here, I have been hanging out mostly with Avani, who is back from the powwow trails for the summer. I love listening to all her stories. We didn't see a lot of each other when I lived here, but I know I'll be missing her, too.

I really should write a letter to Arya before I go though. Tell her all about the Eden mystery. That's what I will title my letter . . . later.

Backyard Mystery!

THE LAST BAG IS INSIDE, AND THE magazine is in its spot. Perfect. I wonder what Eden has been up to all day?

"Kôhkom!" I holler out while she's emptying the bags. "I am heading to Eden's!" She doesn't seem to hear me because she is excitedly talking on the phone to someone in Cree while putting away the groceries. I shrug my shoulders and close the front door behind me. She must be talking about something important if it's taking her away from the usual routine. Kôhkom often tells me on the trip home that she's had enough talking for one day, so she doesn't usually answer the phone on a town day.

Maybe I should wait and ask her what's going on before I go to Eden's. Maybe she didn't hear me . . .

I climb onto the bench and peek through the window. I see Kôhkom still talking excitedly into the phone.

It's weird. My cheeks are getting warm and my eyebrows are squeezing together. I REALLY want to know what she is saying in our language. She knows I can't understand her . . .

Avani has come back from the powwow trail with a bunch of new words in Cree. She can talk to my kôhkom and that's not fair. I want to learn more than the animal names I remember. But I guess I haven't really asked about that this summer either . . .

Why can't I live in both places at the same time?

"Ugh, life isn't fair!" I say out loud to no one as I head to the porch steps.

It doesn't sound like Kôhkom is going to hang up anytime soon. I guess I will go and look for Eden and Avani.

When I turn the corner to use the path between our houses, I see something very big in the yard blocking it. I stop and stare, standing in front of a shadow that stretches to the tips of my toes.

"Wow!" I gasp.

It takes up most of the grassy area. It's so tall!

At least four of me standing on top of my head, maybe more.

"Kôhkom? What is this . . ." I say under my breath.

I wonder if this is connected to the Eden mystery?

Don't Panic, Kôhkom's Got Bannock

I STAND AT THE BOTTOM OF A VERY tall cone wrapped with a light-tan fabric. I touch it. It's soft but I don't know what it is. It kinda feels like my backpack. There are wooden poles sticking out of the top of it and pegs fastening the fabric to the ground. It's glowing in the summer sun hovering over us.

"Whoa, this is amazing . . ." I say to a squirrel who stops to watch me. "Why does this look sort of familiar?"

The anikwacās responds by racing up a tree beside me.

"I don't know either. But come on, what is this?" I say as I walk around it. "There must be an entrance somewhere . . ."

Kôhkom never mentioned anything new on our trip into town. In fact, when we were driving away she said, "Isn't it wonderful how the world stands still here, Sarah?" I knew it was going to be the last trip to town with Kôhkom since the summer breeze is starting to cool and the sun sets earlier. The season is changing so I know school is starting soon.

I look over my shoulder and see that the berry bushes look the same and the laundry is still hanging on the line. But I think the world moved a whole lot today. It moved a whole . . . house?

"Sarah! Sarah Saskatoon Berry! Are you still here?" Kôhkom calls out.

I see what looks like an entrance just as I hear my name being called from the front of the house.

"Kôhkom!" I say as I run to the front of the house. I see her sitting on the porch with the new magazine open on her lap. Her face doesn't show even a little bit of surprise. My face probably has "shock" and "awe" scrawled across it.

"What is that?" I ask, pointing toward the

14

backyard. I lean over, put my hands on my legs, and catch my breath.

Kôhkom points with her lips to the bannock on the table.

"Bannock!" She starts giggling and picks one up.

"Oh Kôhkom! Come on, in the backyard!" I laugh a little but I can feel my eyes widening. This makes Kôhkom giggle even harder as she takes another bite. I pick up a warm piece of bannock and dip it in the jelly on the plate she has set out for me. As always, I know a story is coming by the way Kôhkom places the magazine on the bench beside her. I am ready to be Sarah Ponakey, Storycatcher.

Mystery Solved?

KÔHKOM IS ABOUT TO START HER STORY when we hear voices coming from around the side of the house.

"Who could that be?" Kôhkom asks as she winks at me. "I will get us some extra napkins." She goes inside humming under her breath and I can only guess who it is . . .

"Sarah From the City! I couldn't wait any longer

for you to come and get me, even though my mom kept telling me to give you a chance to arrive and . . . you know, look around," Eden says while motioning her head toward the backyard. Her cousin Avani's eyes widen as she takes a piece of bannock and tries not to laugh at how silly Eden is being.

"Do you know what's in the yard?!" I ask excitedly. Avani nods at me while taking the last bite of a piece of bannock and reaching for another. Eden grabs a large bannock and dips it into the last of my jelly.

"So," Avani and Eden say at the same time.

Eden looks over at her.

"Holy—okay, okay . . ." Avani shrugs her shoulders and goes to the berry bushes to pick the last of the summer berries. You can tell that Avani and Eden are related by the amount of talking they both do! Especially if it is on a topic they are researching, then they'll use every big word possible. Like, *wind turbines* for an energy project they want to bring to the woods. I usually listen and shrug when they ask what I think.

"So, your kôhkom is amazing—but of course you already know that, Sarah. She is always helping us all with something, so the community has been working with my family to help build the tipi to gift to her!"

"WHAT?! How did you not tell me anything all summer, Eden?" My body tenses up. How could she keep this from me? I am her best friend and that is my kôhkom. I take a deep breath. This new feeling is coming back up from my belly. I feel . . . betrayed? One of the latest words taught to me by Eden.

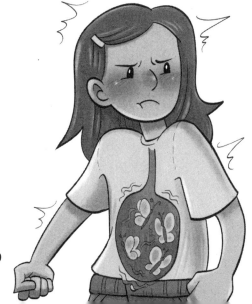

Avani turns to look at me. I can feel my face turn the same color as the berry jam. "I can't believe you kept this a surprise for so long!" I say while staring at my feet. I feel embarrassed for being like this, but also hurt that both Eden and Avani didn't tell me what they have been doing.

Eden was the first one to hear about the magic of attending my first powwow in the woods and all of the beautiful regalia. When I went on my adventure with Âhâsiw, I told her right after my video call with Kôhkom and Mom. I could have kept this a surprise for Kôhkom . . . I think?

I feel my eyes start to well up with tears.

I feel so happy that Kôhkom received such an amazing gift and, at the same time, so sad that my friends didn't tell me. I know I can feel these at the same time. I try to move past it by taking a big deep breath in and a slow breath out, just like Mom showed me.

"Hey Sarah"—Eden dips down so her face is below mine—"I thought you'd really like this surprise too. We wanted to give back to Kôhkom. We know she used to have one way back in the day so . . . Have you looked inside yet?" Eden asks with a worried face.

"Not yet, I wasn't sure what it was. Can I just go inside? Is this why you have been disappearing so much lately?" I shake my head and blink back the tears.

Eden nods at me and gives me a big hug.

So this is why Eden has been acting so differently!

Mystery solved?

"It's taken a lot of time for us to get it just right. We had to find the best trees for the poles and learn to smooth them out! I didn't think it would be that hard with all these trees around here, but it was," Eden says.

"That was my favorite part. Tree hunting!" Avani cuts in.

I'm not sure why I am feeling so sad while they tell me. It wasn't like they were keeping this surprise from me to be mean, but it still hurts. I am the last to learn my language, last to know about the tipi, last to be *in* a tipi . . .

"Let's go!" Eden says, pulling me along while Avani follows.

Mystery Solved

I AM SO HAPPY TO EXPLORE THE TIPI that for a minute I nearly forget to feel jealous about being the last to know about it.

I exhale loudly and Avani puts her hand on my shoulder. I turn around to look at her and she gives me a big smile.

I follow Eden inside. I realize I have seen some tipis in pictures at Kôhkom's house and in books, but I didn't really know what they were. I never thought to ask. And now here I am, inside of one.

"Wow." My mouth drops open.

"Very wow," Avani says, smiling toward the opening at the top.

With the sun shining through the material that wraps around me, it's still bright inside. It smells like the earth and the woods. I am surrounded by what feels like a giant hug—even though it would take at least four of me lying down to reach the other side. If Eden stood on Avani's shoulders and I stood on Eden's shoulders, I might be able to peek outside the opening at the top where the long, smooth poles are tied together and exit.

"Spectacular!" I say as I stare with Avani at the opening way above us. One of the words Eden used in her last letter to me!

"Isn't it?" Eden nudges me and smiles. "This is the first time I helped the community set one up. I have been inside a tipi before on the powwow trail, but not this size!"

"Yeah, I helped build a tipi for the school last year and then this one too," Avani says. "Mom said we can have one soon—I'll probably help build that one too. You should come back for that, Sarah."

I feel the jealousy return. I wish I had the same experiences as Eden and Avani. It's not fair that they are learning so much more than me, AND without me, AND they kept this surprise from me the whole time I have been here. As I walk around looking at the walls and the very tall wooden poles, my foot bumps something on the floor. There was so much to stare at above me that I forgot to look down . . .

"Eeeeep!" squeals Eden.

"Our sleeping bags and backpacks are in here?" I ask with wide eyes. Avani covers her mouth to try and hold back her giggling.

"Mom and I put your sleeping bags in here earlier today," Avani responds. Eden says something back to Avani in Cree.

I wish I understood the language. I will have to remember to ask Kôhkom next time we hang out to teach me more.

"Hiy hiy!" Eden shrieks and hugs me.

"Thank you," I say quietly in English, not sure I'd pronounce it right anyway. I've felt too shy to ask Avani or Eden about our language. I think about my time with Âhâsiw at the forest powwow . . . he would say I need to enjoy the moment. Or at least I should try and do that . . .

I look up to see Eden grinning with wide eyes and reach out to grab her hands. I start jumping around excitedly and I pull her into a circle. She can't help but join in.

"SLEEPOVER!" we shout together. Avani covers her ears and shakes her head at us.

"She thought you two would want to have a sleepover in it tonight. We brought some of your favorite things as a surprise while Eden was keeping herself busy counting down your return . . ." Avani smiles at Eden.

"Awww, thank you, Avani!" we say together and run over to give her a hug.

"Okay, okay, you two!" Avani laughs and ducks out of the hug.

Avani points to Âhâsiw who is beside my sleeping bag.

"Don't worry, Eden, I remembered your toy maskwa," Avani says as she runs to the other side of the tipi giggling.

"Not a toy." Eden glares at Avani and puts her hands on her hips.

"Yeah, not a toy." I glare too with my hands on my hips.

"Okay, okay . . ." Avani says with a playful shrug and throws her hands up in the air. "I forgot . . ."

Eden throws a pillow playfully at Avani and says something in our language. Avani catches it and laughs.

I know one day I will be able to join in. I look at Âhâsiw sitting on my sleeping bag and smile.

It is impressive that Avani managed to keep the sleepover from us. She loves to tell us everything!

"Hey Avani, do you know how to say tipi in our language?" I ask, trying to push my jealousy away.

"Mikiwap," Avani says without turning around.

"Mikiwap," Eden copies and nods at me.

I blush and put my head down, feeling too shy to repeat after them.

I feel my stomach do a flip-flop and decide to look around at everything. I feel very small.

Looking up through the opening from way down here, I can see the clouds slowly moving by. The covering is a light-tan color and is sewn together. I run my fingers over the stitches.

"What's this made of?" I ask no one in particular.

"Canvas," Eden responds as she sets up her sleeping bag.

The wrapping is pulled tight and I kneel down to get a closer look at the pegs holding the fabric to the ground. This is all so magnificent. I roll out my sleeping bag and sit down. I take a deep breath in and slowly let it out.

"So beautiful," I say.

"Katawasisin . . ." Eden and Avani say together.

I feel my shoulders slump and my head drop.

I NEED to ask Kôhkom if we can speak the language together next time I see her.

"Thanks," I say and lie back on my sleeping bag holding Âhâsiw up in the air. He reminds me that life has many surprises—like our powwow adventure in the woods at night. This time it's a tipi beside the trees!

Shadow Puppets and Kindling!

"*ISN'T THIS EXCITING, SARAH?!* I haven't slept in a tipi before. But I can't believe it's our last days together . . ." Eden's voice trails off.

I nod at Eden, but I feel my belly doing those somersaults again. Shouldn't I be happy? I feel kinda lonely, even though I am surrounded by people that care about me.

"Tansi' everyone." We turn to see Kôhkom's

head pop in through the entrance with a bag slung over her shoulder.

I know that bag.

We all know that bag.

It's the thick bag Kôhkom made for us to collect kindling! We were a lot smaller then. Now I know it is made of canvas too, just like the tipi.

"I see you have found an additional surprise, Sarah Saskatoon Berry." Kôhkom smiles at me. "It is getting late and I would like to have a small fire out here. Need some sustenance after this big day," Kôhkom says as she lifts her feet to enter the tipi. I scramble my way up to help her.

"Holy! It's even more magnificent inside, isn't it?" Kôhkom says as she stares up at the opening. I can see her eyes twinkling with the last of the sunlight peeking through the trees.

"I remember my first time looking up at the stars through such an opening. Little bits of smoke would join the clouds and float away together. I laid here dreaming about riding on the smoke like it was a horse traveling across the world. I saw all the great buildings I only ever saw in the library's encyclopedias I looked through every chance I could. I remember my kôhkom singing to me . . ." Her voice begins to waver. I put my hand on her shoulder and smile at her. She lifts the bag off her shoulder.

"I will start getting the kindling," Avani offers as she takes the bag and exits. Kôhkom wipes her eyes on her sleeve and smiles at us. I give Kôhkom a hug.

"Thank you for this wonderful surprise, Kôhkom!" I tell her. "I can't believe I am going to have my first outdoor sleepover with Eden! I love that this is how we're ending summer together." I give Kôhkom a kiss on the cheek and help her leave the tipi as we follow behind.

"I am so grateful to the community for this gift and grateful that you two can have this experience." Kôhkom gives me another squeeze and returns to the house. Kôhkom squeezes are the best.

I love being here and learning about the tipi and being with my best friend. I am really going to miss this, but I miss the city, Mom, and Arya too. I miss Mom's hugs and Arya's jokes. I can't wait to see them again.

"Let's go, Sarah! We have to make the most of tonight." Eden smiles at me and takes the lead toward the edge of the backyard. I can see her smile doesn't look as big as it usually does. Her eyebrows are also close together. She looks a bit sad, actually . . .

"Kîhtwâm ka-wâpamitin!" Eden calls over her shoulder to Kôhkom. She must have seen my face since she responds before I can ask.

"Sorry. I don't mean to make you feel left out. Kôhkom sometimes teaches us when we are at community events and I've been learning a bit when I'm at powwow. Your kôhkom is the coolest. I should ask her if there is a Cree word for coolest . . ." Eden's voice trails off as we enter the darkening woods and Avani hands us each a flashlight from the bag.

I feel . . . sad? Why does she keep things from me? Maybe we aren't as close as I thought. She did apologize to me. Ugh, friendships can feel so confusing! I don't feel like being upset again so I take a deep breath.

I follow slowly behind Eden and Avani, kicking at the dirt clumps and feeling left out. I feel the warm tears slip from my eyes. I'm not sure how I can miss both so much—the city and my community. This is supposed to be a very exciting night but I feel all mixed-up inside.

Then I feel an arm around my shoulders.

"Why so blue, Sarah? This is our first outdoor sleepover!" Eden says, holding the flashlight under her chin and making creepy faces at me.

But before I can answer her, I hear Avani holler toward us.

"Oh my goodness, Eden, your face is scarier than usual," Avani says from across the small clearing.

Eden sticks her tongue out at Avani and squeezes her eyes shut. Avani starts to make a shadow puppet against the tree trunk that is pretending to eat our shadows. I join in and pretend to eat her hands with my shadow puppet.

We burst out laughing and continue to pick up kindling. I forget to respond to Eden and start getting excited about the sleepover again. I bet we could make some fun shadow puppets on the tipi walls.

"Hey, look what I found . . ." Eden whispers as she holds up a slug on a leaf. She knows I see them all the time in the city and love watching the slime trails when I am walking home after school.

"Oooh! I didn't think there would be slugs here!" I rub my eyes in disbelief.

"Does it look like the same kind as in the city? I doubt it. With all the clean air, I bet these wood slugs are ginormous . . ." Eden says as she hands it over to me.

"Kinda, I dunno . . . ?" I say, I'm not sure why she says it like it's a competition.

"Avani," I say, while walking over with the slug, "do you know about slugs?"

Avani stands up from staring at an anthill with her hands on her hips.

"Do I know anything about slugs? Of course I

do. What are your questions?" Avani asks with a grin.

We look at each other with raised eyebrows.

"Well, I didn't think slugs lived in this part of the world. I see them in the city where it is wet, but here . . ." I say, moving the slug toward Avani.

"This is a common European slug," says Avani. "And I must bring it back to my slug container." Avani smiles and hands the kindling bag to Eden then takes the leaf from my hand.

"Slug container?" Eden and I say together, looking at Avani, but Avani is already walking away with it.

"I think I'll name you Sluggarto," Avani says softly into her palm.

Eden shrugs her shoulders and I cover my mouth to hide my giggle.

"Okay, I think we have enough kindling," Eden says. We laugh and Eden puts her arm around my shoulders.

"Sounds good. I can't wait to have this sleepover," I say, trying to forget that I am leaving soon.

"I am going to miss you immensely, Sarah!" Eden responds and I can't help but give her a big squeeze.

I want to stay here forever AND be in the city with Mom and Arya. I wonder if Eden ever feels like this. She always seems calm and cool.

Best Friend Blues

THINGS CAN BE DIFFERENT AND STILL be okay. I learned this while in the city and on my adventure with Âhâsiw. I knew it was going to be different here. Maybe I'm feeling like this because I am heading back to the city soon.

I accidentally let out a big sigh before we exit the woods.

"What is it, Sarah?" Eden turns to me.

"Nothing . . ." I cover my face because her flashlight is shining into my eyes. "Hey, lower that already, eh?" I say.

"Have you ever made bannock over a campfire before?" Eden asks with a grin.

"No," I say with a shrug. "We can't have campfires in the city . . ."

Something else I have been missing out on: campfire bannock.

"Too bad. Campfire bannock is the best. We should try it tonight while you're still here, or 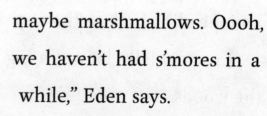 maybe marshmallows. Oooh, we haven't had s'mores in a while," Eden says.

"You're being really

quiet, Sarah." Eden's voice startles me. I was lost in thought.

"Uhh, sorry, Eden," I say quietly. I drop the stick I'm holding and try my best to smile. "I was just . . ."

"Daydreaming? Were you somewhere amazing? My last daydream . . ." Eden starts excitedly telling me all about it, but I zone out and find myself wishing that Arya was here too. She'd be telling us all sorts of knock-knock jokes and making us laugh. She is so funny. I miss that laugh.

I sigh again and Eden scrunches up her face.

"Sarah, what's it like in the city anyway? You haven't said much about it this summer. Why?" Eden stops walking and looks directly at me.

Why is she building tipis?

Why am I not wanting to share about my city life?

Why is she moving on with her life without me?

"Sarah? Hello? Are you feeling okay?" Eden is staring at me with one eyebrow raised.

"Yeah, I just didn't want to be reminded I am leaving soon, I guess." I look up and see Eden nodding.

"I really like hanging out with Arya," I say as I watch Eden pick up the stick I dropped and peel off

little bits of it. I don't know if I should keep talking, but I can't seem to stop myself. And like Arya, I can't seem to stop talking . . .

48

Eden keeps looking down.

"She is hilarious and we play all sorts of games on the playground after school. We go to a coding class on Tuesdays. I think that is something I could really get into. We also started a book club with the two of us on Fridays. Arya has a favorite stuffed animal too and it's an eagle. I wrote to you about that. We laugh a lot. I mean a LOT! I am glad we found each other. I can't wait to write to her and tell her all about the tipi surprise!"

I finally stop myself and look over at Eden. She looks like her eyes are filled with tears. What did I say?

"Cool, good for you," Eden

says. She spins on her heel and walks faster to Kôhkom's house.

Does Eden not understand that I didn't want to talk about the city because it doesn't have her in it? Maybe we are both keeping things from each other that we shouldn't be. I sigh again. This time no one hears me.

Kôhkom's Magic

WHEN WE ARRIVE BACK AT KÔHKOM'S
backyard I can see that she has been busy!

"Hi Sarah!" Avani sees me first as she is just
on the outskirts of the backyard clearing picking
berries.

"Hey Avani! Did you get the slug in your habitat
container all right?" I ask her.

"Yep! And I helped Kôhkom with the food. Why

did Eden come back before you? Did she have to go to the bathroom that badly?" Avani asks with wide eyes as she walks to the picnic table.

I shrug in response and Avani laughs, then turns to finish setting the picnic table. I look to the middle of the yard where the campfire is. Avani must have helped move the table closer to it. The table is full of food that she is arranging. Yum!

Kôhkom has all the fixings for veggie dogs and s'mores. There is also some lemonade and freshly picked berries.

I don't see Eden, but I notice her shoes are kicked off by the back door.

"Tansi' Sarah! Eden went running inside to wash

her hands," Kôhkom says as she pushes around the logs in the fire.

"Okay, Kôhkom!" I wave at her as she puts the roasting sticks by the campfire.

"Soon you won't even need me!" Kôhkom laughs. She motions for me to bring the veggie dog tray from the picnic table to the campfire. Kôhkom has the fire going just right.

"Can we start roasting, Kôhkom?" I ask.

"Yes, yes, of course . . . I am sure Eden will be out any minute. Start one for her as well," Kôhkom says.

Avani walks over to the fire and starts putting veggie dogs on sticks.

Eden comes outside a moment later. Her eyes

look puffy, but she gives me a half-smile and sits on the log across from me.

"Here, Eden." I hand her one of the sticks Avani prepared and pick up another one.

"Thanks," she says quietly.

"I think you are ready for a story." Kôhkom joins us by the fire.

I can feel my eyes widen along with my smile and look up to see Eden smiling up at her too. I think Kôhkom is magical—the shadows she casts against the tipi walls make her look like she is much taller than she is. She sits in her favorite camping chair.

Kôhkom takes some time to reflect and get comfortable while looking at the tipi.

I sit on the ground and lean against a log to

get comfortable too. I always love story time with Kôhkom.

Tipi Tales

THE SKY IS DARK NOW AND THE sounds change around us. I hear a faraway mêscacâkanis calling out. I guess I do know more words in my language than I think I do . . .

Some of the brightest stars are saying hello as the sun sinks below the horizon. Kôhkom tells us some of her favorite stories about growing up and the old ways. I can tell she is very tired because her words come out slower and slower.

"Now, I am going to tell you one last story and then it is off to bed with you two and home for you, Avani." Kôhkom looks toward us as our eyes start to flutter. It is nice and cozy by the fire.

"Yes, Kôhkom," we say together, and then yawn together too. Kôhkom has been slowly letting the fire go out. I smile at Eden, so excited that we get to have our first sleepover in ages. I hope it's not weird when it's just the two of us tonight. I look over at Kôhkom who covers her mouth as she yawns.

"The tipi has always been a way of life for my parents, and my grandparents, and my great-grandparents. Our ancestors built these as homes." Kôhkom stares at the tipi and we all follow her gaze.

"Kôhkom, did you live in one?" I ask.

"No, but I do remember staying in one when I was little. I remember the blankets piled up and the sounds of laughter outside . . ." Kôhkom's voice drifts off.

"The tipi, or mikiwap, is made with lots of thought, and each pole represents a teaching. We make sure the entrance points east so that—when we are inside, and when we exit—there is always a renewal, or a new beginning, with each sunrise. The tipi used to be much smaller since we moved around a lot and the wrap was made from animal hides. Now we use canvas, so they can be much bigger." Kôhkom's voice quiets and her eyes are slowly closing.

"Do you want me to get you some tea, Kôhkom?" I ask. "Or your favorite blanket?"

"Oh, thank you, Sarah Saskatoon Berry. I will finish up and then I will go to sleep. I remember one night we were sleeping under an amazing star show. I could hear drumming and singing in the distance. My older sisters were still dancing, but I was with Mom who was humming quietly to me in the tipi. She told me the stars told the best bedtime stories, which is why the moon is never lonely. That night, I remember dreaming about a wâposos visiting me. We hopped all around the forest together as she taught me about the plants I could use for medicine.

Ahh, Wâposos, she visited me often in my dreams," Kôhkom finishes, stretching her arms out.

"Like Âhâsiw came to me!" I say excitedly. I can see Eden looking at me with a raised eyebrow.

Kôhkom nods then says, "The stars are looking very bright tonight so I think your sleepover will have some great stories." Kôhkom smiles at us and hands me the electric lantern sitting by her feet.

"I am so excited! I am not sure if I am ever going to fall asleep, Sarah." Eden laughs as she tries to stop herself from yawning.

"I wonder what stories the stars will tell us tonight. You always love a good story," I say to Eden while nudging her with my elbow. We enter the tipi giggling and tripping over one another.

"Goodnight, Kôhkom! Goodnight, everyone!" we say together while we look for our pajamas.

We can hear Avani bringing in the last items from around the campfire for Kôhkom as we crawl into our sleeping bags.

"Kîhtwâm ka-wâpamitin," Avani says as she walks past the opening and onto the short path home. "Enjoy the maskwak!" Avani hollers over her shoulder.

"Aiii, you . . ." we hear Kôhkom say, and we all laugh.

"Don't pay her any attention, girls. Goodnight, sleep well!" Kôhkom says as she blows us kisses and closes the tipi flap.

It suddenly feels very dark, even with the

lantern we brought into the tipi, and I reach around my pillow for Âhâsiw.

"Sarah?" Eden whispers.

"Yeah?" I say even quieter.

"Are you scared?" she asks. I can hear her reaching around in her backpack.

"Not really. I am glad I have you and Âhâsiw here," I say quietly as I lift him above my head and pretend he is flying above me. I wonder if he has ever slept in a tipi before.

"Are you scared?" I ask. I know I wouldn't be able to sleep without Âhâsiw.

Eden doesn't answer me and I can hear some rustling sounds. "Where's my maskwa? I can't find her anywhere." Eden sounds worried.

"It has to be here. Your mom and Avani know you need her to sleep. I bet she double-checked . . ." I say as I reach for the lantern and point it closer to Eden. Her eyes are starting to fill with tears and she has dumped her backpack onto her sleeping bag. I know exactly how Eden is feeling: scared. Just like that time I accidentally dropped Âhâsiw outside and Arya found him.

I crawl toward her sleeping bag to help her look for Maskwa.

"We will find her," I say, hopeful.

Eden doesn't respond.

Missing Maskwa

EDEN HAS TEARS STREAMING DOWN her face.

"I won't be able to sleep without my maskwa, Sarah," Eden says softly.

What would Kôhkom do to make me feel comfortable?

"Eden, here, have Âhâsiw tonight." I hold him out toward Eden, but she slowly shakes her head no and hangs her head down.

Hmmm, it's not very often I am the one cheering up Eden! She has always enjoyed my stories about the adventures with Âhâsiw so maybe I'll try that.

"Hey, Eden, remember when I told you about the adventures with Âhâsiw and he met the maskwak for the first time? They were so huge and sat on teeny, tiny chairs. Oh, and the vests they wore . . . wait a minute . . ." I stop to think back. I hear Eden sniffle a bit.

"What?" she says quietly.

"Doesn't YOUR maskwa wear a vest? With red beads?" I stand up quickly with wide eyes.

"EDEN," I say excitedly. "Do you think your

maskwa was at the powwow in the woods with me? Maybe she is out there in the woods drumming for a powwow." I can hear her starting to giggle now as she sniffles back some tears.

"Come on, Sarah," Eden says with a sigh as she stands up in front of me. "There is no way Maskwa is out there drumming. First of all, I have taken her to plenty of powwows and never once did she join in."

"Eden, magical things have happened before," I say while tapping my foot and crossing my arms.

"Okay, but it was also just, like, a dream. It wasn't real," Eden says with her arms crossed.

I am hurt that she doesn't think it was all real

for me. I feel the butterflies and flip-flops in my belly growing bigger. How could my best friend not believe me?

"REALLY, EDEN? You're my bestest friend in the whole wide world and YOU don't believe my adventures? Have you ever believed me?" I feel my jaw drop to the floor.

"You think your stuffed animal REALLY came to life and took you on an adventure?" Eden says and sits down with her back to me.

"UN-BE-LIEV-ABLE," I say. My best friend. My bosom buddy. The one I can tell all my secrets to. One of my biggest life adventures and all this time she thought it was just a story? Who is she? What happened to the Eden I know?

I close my mouth and take a deep breath. What else am I going to do? We are stuck here together until the sun comes up. Then we can go our separate ways. FOREVER.

I sit down hard on my sleeping bag and turn my back to her. The shadows on the tipi walls from the lantern make me look like a giant maskwa. I start to move my arms in the air and growl. I look over my shoulder and see that Eden is starting to make animal shadow puppets.

"Humph," I say. I can't believe she is playing and doesn't seem even a little bit sorry for what she said to me.

"Humph?" Eden says to the tipi wall.

"Yeah. You don't even seem like you care about how I feel," I say.

"Yeah, well neither do you!" Eden responds.

"What are you talking about?" I turn to her, confused.

"First, you leave me. Fine. You have to go. I have to figure out this whole new way of life without you. Second, you start writing to me about a new friend, Arya. Okay, fine, I know things are going to be different. I am learning these things I thought we would learn together forever, but you're not here, Sarah." Eden's face isn't as scrunched up anymore and she looks sad again. I didn't know SHE felt this way too! She's Eden. She usually dusts off her knees when she falls down and keeps going. I'm not used to seeing her cry.

"But that's what I feel like too!" I say. "I had to move away from you and figure out all these new things and find new people to talk to. I didn't know anyone at all. I thought we would be learning everything together forever too," I reply sadly.

"But you sound like you're doing so much and have forgotten me here," Eden says to me while staring at the ground.

"I could never forget about you! You're my best friend and you'll be in my life forever and ever," I say and walk over to her. "Plus, I thought you were moving on in your life without me! Look at all the amazing things you get to do that I don't." I twirl with my arms wide open and I bump into her while I do.

"Oops, sorry," I say quietly. But Eden smiles, stands up, and gives me a hug.

"Your shadow looked like a ballerina maskwa!" Eden giggles and then lifts her arms up again.

I laugh and lift my arms up to join her as we dance around the tipi. Then we hear a noise outside. It sounds like branches cracking in the woods.

"MASKWA!" we yell together and dive into our sleeping bags.

Maskwa, Is That You?

IN THE MIDDLE OF OUR SCREAMING we hear laughter coming from outside. We know exactly who it is.

"Avani!" we yell as we throw open our sleeping bags and stomp to the opening. Honestly, cousins can be the worst.

Eden opens the tipi entrance and waves the lantern back and forth.

"Where are you?" she huffs. "You are atrocious!"

I pop my head out beside hers.

"Come out here, you scaredy-cat!" I holler.

"Me?" I can hear the laughter coming closer as Avani pops up from around the tipi.

Eden scrunches her nose at her and shakes her head. "Wait till I tell my mom."

"Yeah, yeah, she's the one who sent me down here to make sure you had your precious maskwa . . . I guess it fell out when I was packing for you earlier," Avani says as she throws the stuffed bear over to Eden. "Y'all have a good sleep now, ya hear?" She laughs as she turns on the flashlight and heads back on the trail to their house.

74

"You really can be wretched!" Eden hollers at her, but this time with a smile. "And THANK YOU!" We return to our sleeping bags and click off the lantern.

"Okay, she may not always be the worst . . ." Eden is speaking to Maskwa more than to me.

"I can't believe her sometimes," I say as I hug Âhâsiw and stifle a yawn.

"I didn't mean what I said earlier," Eden says quietly. "You know, about the adventure you had with Âhâsiw. I miss you so much. Some days I can't stop thinking about what you are doing in the big city. How lucky you are to be there and exploring a new place while I am here doing all the same things we have always done."

I can hear Eden let out a big sigh.

"It's different," I tell her. "But I want you to always know that I think about you and I hope you're having fun too. How about we write more about the amazing things we are doing and then we can start a list of adventures for next time I visit?"

"I love that idea," Eden says excitedly. "Yes! Maybe I won't get all these butterflies in my stomach when I hear about your city adventures."

I can hear Eden sitting up in her sleeping bag.

"You get those too?" I say as I sit up quickly, shocked. "I thought it was just me!"

"I think we might be living far apart, but we are still the same Sarah and Eden," Eden says, with a yawn. I can hear her lying back down so I do too and begin to feel very sleepy.

"Kinda like when I came back from town and a lot was the same except the tipi," I say.

"I am so glad you're my best friend, Sarah," Eden says right before I hear snoring.

"I am so glad you're mine too, Eden," I reply softly, knowing she's fast asleep.

Tansi' Maskwa

I AM WOKEN UP BY EDEN SHAKING MY shoulders.

"Wake up! Do you hear that?" Eden whispers.

I rub my eyes and sit up.

"What am I supposed to be hearing?" I ask Eden.

"Listen, Sarah!" Eden spits out urgently.

I am not entirely sure what she expects to hear

from the woods in the middle of the night. Maybe Avani is back for round two of scaring us?

Then I hear it.

Booom . . .

Boooom . . .

Booooom . . .

My body tingles from nose to toes. I feel the same way I did the first time I heard drumming, and I put my hands over my heart.

"That's the same powwow song I heard before in the woods with Âhâsiw," I whisper.

We turn our heads toward the singing. It can't be. My eyes grow wider and I look for Ahâsiw. He is still stuffed and lying beside me. Hmmm . . .

"Who would be singing in the middle of the night in the woods?" Eden asks, concerned.

I am fully awake now. The singing is beautiful and feels like another warm hug. I begin to sway as the singing grows closer and closer.

"It's beautiful, the voice. I have heard this singing before," Eden says, and she starts to relax.

Then we both hear steps by the entrance of the tipi.

"Tansi' Eden, tansi' Sarah . . ." a friendly voice greets us from outside of the entrance.

"Who's there?" asks Eden confidently.

"Maskwa," the voice responds playfully.

We both look over at Eden's sleeping bag to where Maskwa was lying. She is missing again.

Then we turn to each other with our mouths open.

"Sarah . . ." Eden whispers. "I can't believe this."

"Coming!" I say with a big smile and take Eden's hand. "Come on, Eden. Trust me!"

"Tansi' Eden and Sarah," Maskwa bellows out at us when we exit the tipi.

We raise our eyes up to her, then to each other, and then back up to her. She is huge and looks so cuddly. She is wearing a bright, beautiful vest with red beading. It looks snug on her. She is magnificent and has the warmest smile.

"Can I give you both a hug?" Maskwa asks us.

"Of course!" we say together.

She wraps us in her arms and gives us the best

bear hug. I can see where the name for that comes from. She's so strong!

"Wow, Sarah! How is this even happening right now?" Eden asks in disbelief. She is walking around Maskwa who has now bent down to look at us.

Eden touches her big bear paw then cups her cheeks between her palms and squishes Maskwa's face a little—just like she does with her small stuffed animal.

"But how . . ." Eden's voice trails off.

I know that Eden likes to read a lot and learn about everything so she can understand the world. Maybe that's why she couldn't quite understand my adventure with Âhâsiw. Sometimes I forget how differently we think and see things. I guess that's what makes us great friends.

We both look up at Maskwa as she stands up straight again and starts laughing. We join in. I can't believe we have Eden's maskwa standing here with us!

Magic Under the Stars

MASKWA SITS DOWN BY THE CAMPFIRE, which has magically relit. Smoke rises in gentle puffs going straight up toward the night sky.

Maskwa starts singing quietly and pulls a drum from behind the log she is sitting on. The song is one I heard before with Kôhkom and at the powwow with Ahâsiw. It makes my feet tap. I can see Eden's feet tapping along as well.

We listen until Eden and I join in. I didn't know I could sing, but somehow, like magic, we are all in unison. Eden and I look at each other with big smiles. The three of us stand together watching the rising smoke. It smells like sweetgrass and sage.

Maskwa winds down the drumming and puts her beautiful hand drum back in the beaded bag on the log before sitting back down beside it.

The smoke billows upward and surrounds us once again like it did earlier when Kôhkom and Avani were with us. We follow Maskwa's lead and sit down on the logs side by side. We watch the fire in silence for a while and hear an owl hooting.

"I have so many questions," Eden says.

"Me too!" I say with a laugh.

Maskwa looks at us and winks.

"Oh, I bet you do!" She lets out a loud laugh.

Eden and I look at each other with wide eyes. She pinches herself and winces. I try to hold back a laugh.

"I know you two haven't been getting along lately. There are a lot of changes but I want you to remember something: no matter where you are in the world, you two will always be right here." Maskwa pats her head with her giant paw. We let out a little giggle and pat one another's heads.

"Yes, Maskwa, but it's not fair that Sarah gets to experience so many new things without me. I want to be right there with her, always, not just in our imaginations," Eden says with a pout.

"And I always want to be with Eden here. Where nothing changes! I am so sad and also so happy for Eden, but I don't want to be too happy," I say gently.

"It is tough when there are big changes in our lives, but nothing ever stays the same," Maskwa explains. "We grow, we adapt, we change, we learn new things, and isn't that the fun of life? Look at you two tonight. If everything stayed the same we wouldn't be here. Would we?"

Maskwa smiles at us while she opens her arms up to the sky.

"Your stories and who you are will always be with you. That will never change. Just like this mikiwap here. It brought you two together when you felt different, separated, in the woods earlier. It is through learning your traditions and culture— and sharing your experiences with one another— that you can grow forward." Maskwa closes her eyes. Then she shifts in her seat, nearly falling off and startling herself. I think she must be getting tired. I can see that the sky is starting to become lighter and lighter.

"Mmm, yes, girls. You see, it is important to tell one another stories just like you do with your letters. Keep sharing and staying connected. Life and friendships change and grow with time, but it's how you view the world that will help you. Know that when you close your eyes and imagine one another, you are there. Always. Just like your ancestors who built these tipis and traveled all over. Not always together, but always connected with one another through who we are." Maskwa stretches.

"I don't want you to go, but like you say, if we close our eyes and remember you, we will be connected." Eden smiles at Maskwa.

"Plus, I am usually close by . . ." Maskwa lets out another loud laugh.

She gently places the drum bag over her shoulder.

"It is time for you two to rest and for me to say goodnight." Maskwa stands up and stretches. She looks as tall as the tipi!

"I am so happy we were able to see you tonight, Maskwa. So happy to be with my two bestest friends in the whole wide world. Next time we need to let Âhâsiw know," Eden says, and giggles.

"That would be AMAZING!" I squeal with delight. I haven't seen Eden this happy all summer!

"Off to bed, little ones." Maskwa takes our hands in her paws and walks us to the tipi opening.

We give Maskwa one more big hug and giggle as we climb into our sleeping bags.

"Bye, Maskwa! Hiy hiy!" we say.

"Until next time, Eden and Sarah. Sweet dreams." Maskwa closes the tipi flap. We hear her singing as she returns to the woods.

"I just get really sad sometimes when I think about everything we do separately now," Eden says quietly as she snuggles into her sleeping bag.

"Me too. But I am so grateful that we get to have this night forever and ever in our memories," I say to Eden as I burrow deeper into my sleeping bag. I look over and see that she is starting to fall asleep.

"I am so glad you came back this summer, Sarah. I hope I can visit you in the city next summer," Eden says.

I hear Eden's snoring. How does she fall asleep so quickly?

Storycatching at Breakfast

I WAKE UP TO THE SOUND OF BIRD songs and talking close by. Kôhkom must already be in the garden. It's warm and cozy in the tipi, so it's tough to get up. Eden must have heard the same sounds. She rolls over toward me.

"Hi Eden!" I cover my mouth and giggle at Eden's morning face. She moves around a lot so her hair sticks up everywhere. She curls up tightly with her maskwa and there is a mark on her cheek from the toy. She sticks her tongue out at me. We both stop talking for a minute as we hear quiet voices and movement outside.

"Who do you think is out there?" Eden asks.

"Aiii, hmmm . . . Maskwa?!" I laugh with Eden.

"Do you think that was real?" Eden looks at me seriously.

"Definitely," I say with a big smile.

We hear footsteps approaching and giggles. We know those giggles . . .

"Hi Avani!" Eden looks at me and shakes her head. Her cousin is always close by—especially when we are doing something extra cool, like this.

"Hiiiii," Avani says as she opens the flap and pops her head in. "Kôhkom made breakfast, and your mom is here to join us, Eden. They asked me to come and get you."

"Okay, okay, we're coming . . ." I stand up and stretch.

"Coming, Eden?" I look back to see Eden hugging Maskwa and speaking softly in her ear. She looks over and blushes when she sees I am watching her.

"Yep, coming," Eden says quietly as she jumps up to follow us out.

I smell breakfast before I get inside the house. Berries, bannock, and oatmeal!

"Hi girls!" Eden's mom, standing by the door

to help bring breakfast to the table, opens her arms to give us a big hug. "I am here to help Kôhkom and to bring home the sleepover gear."

"Go wash up first and join us for breakfast," Kôhkom says and waves us toward the sink.

Eden and I rush back to the table.

"Kôhkom," I say. "Guess what?"

Kôhkom sits down at the end of the table, her usual spot, and looks up from her tea with a smile.

"Mmm, Sarah, we want to hear all about your night. Tell us," Kôhkom says while Eden's mom takes a seat across from Avani with her tea.

"Yes, how was your night in the tipi?" Eden's mom asks with a wink and smile a to Kôhkom.

"Maskwa, Eden's stuffie, came to visit us—like Âhâsiw! She has a beautiful voice and a drum. She sang to us! Then told us about how we will always be connected and—" I start to say.

Avani has dropped her spoon and is staring at us in disbelief. Kôhkom wipes her mouth and puts her mug on the table. Eden's mom sets her mug down too. They both look toward us.

"Oh, she did? That sounds like a wonderful night in the tipi," Kôhkom says with a smile. "Tell us more." She takes another sip of tea and sits back. Everyone's eyes are on Eden and me.

"Go on, Eden!" I nod over to her as she always loves to tell a good story.

Eden hops down from her chair and stands up to tell us all about Maskwa coming to visit us. She's so funny and is such a great storyteller. We all join her when she starts dancing and singing around the table.

Everyone is grinning after Eden finishes telling us all about the adventure with Maskwa. While

Kôhkom, Eden's mom, and Avani start eating again, I whisper to Eden.

"We will always have the night in the tipi with Maskwa! No matter where we are. Always connected." Eden hugs me.

"Forever," Eden says.

"Always," I reply.

Kôhkom stands up and walks toward me and hugs me gently from behind.

"Sarah Saskatoon Berry, stories and adventures always come when we need them most. Trust the timing of the world." Kôhkom slowly turns toward the table.

"Now, all of you, I think we need to go to the river today and see how the berries are down there. My bushes are looking sparse for some reason . . ." Kôhkom winks toward us and moves to clear her plate. Avani is one step ahead of her and takes her plate to put in the dishwasher. She and Eden's mom are still eating breakfast and speaking together in Cree. I can't wait to learn more!

"Kôhkom, can I please write a letter first? I want to tell Arya all about what happened before I forget," I say. Then I have a brilliant idea and ask Eden, "Want to write the letter with me?"

"Yes, yes, go, go . . ." Kôhkom smiles toward us while she helps Avani with another helping of berries in her oatmeal.

"How about I draw her a picture of Maskwa and us?" Eden suggests.

"Yes! Arya would love that!" I say.

Dearest Arya!

I am writing this letter and Eden drew the picture of our night in the tipi (or mikiwap)! She is such a great drawer. I wanted to tell you all about our visit with Maskwa and I couldn't wait until I got home. We had a phenomenal experience with Maskwa (phenomenal is a new word Eden taught me!). She visited with us, just like Âhâsiw.

Have you ever slept in a tipi? It was our first sleepover in one!!

So I guess to answer your question, yes, we saw a maskwa in the woods!

When I'm back in the city, I can't wait to show you some of the dancing we did around the campfire.

102

I think you need to come and visit. There are so many cool things to do here!

I miss you and can't wait to see you again soon.

Countdown to the city is on. I am going to go on a few more adventures with Eden and I can't wait to tell you all about it.

Your Friend,

Sarah

P.S.: Hi Arya, I can't wait to meet you. I hope you can come out here or I can come and hang out with you two in the city! I hope you like the picture I drew! —Eden.

Dearest Arya!

I am writing this letter and Eden drew the picture of our night in the tipi (or mikiwap)! She is such a great drawer.

I wanted to tell you all about our visit with Maskwa and I couldn't wait until I got home. We had a _phenomenal_ experience with Maskwa (phenomenal is a new word Eden taught me!). She visited with us, just like Âtâsiw.

Have you ever slept in a tipi? It was our first sleepover in one!! So I guess to answer your question, yes, we saw a Maskwa in the woods!

When I'm back in the city, I can't wait to show you some of the dancing we did around the campfire. I think you need to come and visit. There are so many cool things to do here!

AUTHOR'S NOTE

TANSI', HELLO! THANKS FOR SPENDING time with Sarah Ponakey and her friends as they go on a new adventure. Even though Sarah now lives in the city, she had a lot of fun visiting Kôhkom, Eden, and Avani in the woods during the summer break!

I moved to a new place away from my grandmother when I was young, and I remember how tough it was. We didn't have the same opportunities as we do today to stay connected.

I am First Nations and Scottish and grew up mostly in British Columbia. I learned about First Nations culture while making connections as a university student. I can relate to Sarah because I felt like I didn't know what to do and like I didn't have much cultural knowledge when it seemed others knew so much! But, as with Sarah, so many kind people in the world showed up and helped me along the way.

I hope you enjoyed sounding out the Cree words. It's fun learning new things, and I thought it would be good for us to learn some of the Cree language together while reading about Sarah's adventures.

Thank you for reading this book. I hope you had a great time with Sarah and Maskwa at the campfire. I wonder what Sarah will get up to next . . .

Sita

ACKN⊕WLEDGMENTS

Thank you to my family for conversations during family gatherings. A big thank you to my sister Gopala Metatawabin and brother-in-law Shannin Metatawabin for our ongoing discussions and your support in the book writing world. Thank you to my parents for believing in me as I worked toward becoming an author since I was a youth. Our gatherings interspersed with questions and comments on tipis and family connections have created a deeper bond.

Big hugs to my husband, Gord, who helps behind the scenes so I can write uninterrupted. Much love to my children Arya, Avani, and Anjali who have been cheering me on since I wrote my first adventure with Sarah. I am so grateful to them for providing me with their thoughts throughout the writing of this story for you.

Thank you to the entire Annick Press team for believing in this dream I had for Sarah. Especially to my editor Stephanie Myers who has worked alongside me with such dedication to bring this book out into the world. Thank you to illustrator Azby who brought Sarah, friends, and family to the page in such a beautiful way. As well, a big thank you, hiy hiy, to Dorothy Visser who reviewed the Cree words you see throughout the book. I am so very grateful.

With gratitude to my friends far and wide for

eagerly supporting and cheering me on through this process. I'm so happy to have received kind words of encouragement from fellow writers, authors, and new friends I have met along the way. You have helped me more than you'll ever know.

Thank you to the writing group in Penticton that first heard my manuscript and supported my goals.

Life is one big adventure. Keep dreaming and believing in the magic.

Thank you,

Sita

Sarah Ponakey, STORYCATCHER

Turn the page for
a sneak peek into
Sarah Ponakey's new
adventure, coming soon!

Dearest Sarah,

Tansi', my best friend from the stars to the inner core of the Earth. I am writing to you from a place of sorrow. I will be away for the next month to visit my family in Montana. We are "extending spring break into a grand spring break." My mom keeps saying this to me, but it won't be.

My cousins are fine, but I won't be able to write to you or get your letters until I am back. Uncle Pete at the post office said he will make sure that your letters aren't lost while I am gone. I asked Mom for a phone, but she said no.

I understand what you said: Life is the pits.

Tell Arya. I am not ignoring anyone, I am with my family.

Next spring break I am going to ask them to drop me off at your place on the way home. You must be somewhere between here and Montana?

Always,

Eden

Yay, Kôhkom
in the City!

I WAKE UP TO THE SMELL OF BREAKFAST
and to this letter from Eden beside my bed.

Âhâsiw didn't even wake me up.

I am sure going to miss Eden's letters, but this
means . . .

"Kôhkom is here!" I holler as I jump out of bed
with Âhâsiw in my hand.

I run down the hall toward the kitchen where I can smell the tea brewing.

"Sarah, what did I tell you about—" Mom says as I run into Kôhkom's outstretched arms. "Never mind." She smiles as she sits down with her mug of tea.

"Sarah Saskatoon Berry. Tell me everything," Kôhkom says with a wink and gives me an extra squeeze. She knows how much I love to talk. I think I talk even more now than I ever did before moving to the city. I have so many questions about everything, and then questions about my questions!

"Kôhkom! When did you arrive? How did you get here? Will you move here? I bet if I asked Arya's parents, they could find you an apartment in the same building. Did the crows outside welcome you when you arrived? Were they sleeping? Did they say good morning to you? Whoops, I forgot to say good morning to them." I stop, take a deep breath, and exhale. "Eden is GONE for a month?!"

Without missing a beat and counting each response on her fingers, Kôhkom replies, "12:45 a.m. Your mom was complaining about staying awake and I tucked her in. I got here on a great carriage flown by multiple birds. They fed me cookies and tea. I bet I could move to the moon if I asked you, but alas, I will stay in the woods. The crows told me that they are very happy I am here and then went back to sleep, but they woke me up singing their good morning song. I sang with them! Eden is gone for a month to her cousins' and she was very sad when she dropped off the letter. I assured her I would hand it over promptly once I arrived. I think I got everything . . ." Kôhkom inhales and taps her fingers on her chin, thinking about the list of questions I asked. I giggle and give Kôhkom a big hug.

"Oh, Mom, I don't know how you remembered all of that!" my mom says, shaking her head and chuckling as she gets up to take the oatmeal off the stove.

"Kôhkom, you've still got it. Now to teach you my new handshake for only the closest of people." I smile as she holds out her hand for a high five, which I can't leave hanging. Âhâsiw gives her one too with his wing.

"Sarah, can you . . ." my mom starts to ask.

"Yes, Mom"—I hop onto the counter to get the

bowls—"I'll set the table. Can I go and get Arya, too? I know she wants to meet Kôhkom!" I jump down and start running to the door past Kôhkom who is happily sitting at the table.

"Not right now, Sarah. Remember the importance of being patient? Your kôhkom has just arrived, so let her get settled," Mom says.

I skid to a halt and spin around. I open my mouth and begin to protest, but Kôhkom beats me to it.

"I look forward to meeting Arya soon, Sarah Saskatoon Berry, but it seems you have forgotten something." Kôhkom smiles at me then nods toward the kitchen counter where the bowls are still sitting with her cup of tea.

I know that look. Oops!

"Yes. Kôhkom," I bring over the bowls to finish setting the table and then I bring Kôhkom her tea. "I really can't wait for you to meet my friend. She's so funny."

"And I will. I have heard so much about her," Kôhkom says.

"If you think I have a lot of energy . . . wait until you meet Arya!" I say in my outside voice.

I hear Kôhkom stifle a giggle as she takes a sip of tea.

"I very much look forward to our visit together. I feel that I am going to learn a lot of new things about the city," Kôhkom says quietly as Mom fills her bowl with oatmeal.

SITA MacMILLAN is a Cree-Scottish author who writes books for children. Much like Sarah, Sita spent a lot of time living in cities and towns as a kid, away from her First Nations community. But unlike Sarah, Sita was already a grown-up when she started reconnecting with her First Nations culture. Sarah and her friends show us that learning about culture is a unique journey for every person. Sita spends a lot of time hanging out and talking with her three kids, painting in her studio, and walking around beautiful Prince Edward Island, Canada's smallest province!

Yannick Dupuis

AZBY WHITECALF is a Plains Cree illustrator who creates dreamy and cozy stories for children and those who are kids at heart. Azby loves to watch fantasy movies about princesses and dragons, but also loves when all the characters are puppets! Being Plains Cree means that Azby is learning their language of Nehiyawak and loves to listen to Cree folklore—especially about Sabe the bigfoot!

Azby likes to spend time with their family and friends, usually swimming in the lake or playing board games. During Azby's time off, you can usually find them immersed in a video game or scouring the art supply store for new things to play with. Clowns are one of Azby's favorite things and they would love to learn magic and how to juggle!